EEK! CREAK! SNICKER, SNEAK

by **Rhonda Gowler Greene**

Illustrated by **Jos. A. Smith**

Atheneum Books for Young Readers   New York London Toronto Sydney Singapore

For my son, Brad, who loves a good book.
　　　　　　　　　　　　　　　—R.G.G.

For Charissa, Kari, Joe, Emily, and Andrea and all
the artists I've had the pleasure of working with
at Pratt.
　　　　　　　　　　　　　　　—J.A.S.

AUTHOR'S NOTE

The words "bugbear" and "bugaboo" are thought to
be of Middle English and Celtic origins, respectively.
In folklore, they mean an "imaginary creature" or
"hobgoblin."　　　　　　　—Rhonda Gowler Greene

ILLUSTRATOR'S NOTE

Some books are more fun for an artist to illustrate than
others. *Eek! Creak! Snicker, Sneak* is definitely one of
the good ones. I prefer to draw from imagination
rather than depend on photographs or posed models for
reference. Bugbear and Bugaboo didn't have to look like
anything anyone has ever seen before, so I could
really go wild. I filled sketchbook pages with little
creatures before the ones you see in this book were
selected.

In my imagination, I tried to picture what Bugbear
and Bugaboo were doing when they made the different
noises, and how much fun they must have been having
while they were making them.

For the finished illustrations, I first drew them
with a light pencil line. Then I colored the pictures
with watercolor, keeping the cool blues and greens
for the nighttime settings and the warm colors (yellow,
orange, and red) for the lamplight. Finally, I added
outlines and details with pen and ink.　　—Jos. A. Smith

Atheneum Books for Young Readers
An imprint of Simon & Schuster Children's Publishing Division
1230 Avenue of the Americas
New York, New York 10020

Book design by Michael Nelson
The text of this book is set in BlockheadUnplugged.
The illustrations are rendered in watercolor, pen, and ink.

Printed in Hong Kong
1 2 3 4 5 6 7 8 9 10

Library of Congress Cataloging-in-Publication Data

Greene, Rhonda Gowler.
Eek! Creak! Snicker, Sneak / by Rhonda Gowler Greene ;
illustrated by Jos. A. Smith.—1st ed.
p.　cm.
Summary: Bugbear and Bugaboo are creatures who like to
play scary tricks on children, until the night they get
scared themselves.

ISBN 0-689-83047-5

[1. Monsters—Fiction. 2. Fear—Fiction. 3. Stories in rhyme.]
I. Smith, Joseph A. (Joseph Anthony), 1936– ill. II. Title.
PZ8.3.G824 Bu 2002
[E]—dc21　　00-045147

FIRST
EDITION

When all the town is fast asleep,
two little creatures crawl and creep
up the hill,
over the top,
down again,
then—PLOP—they stop.

Bugbear giggles, "Tee-hee-hee-hee!"

He loves to frighten you and me

with EEEKS and CR-R-REAKS and big, bad H-OW-OWLS

and tiny SQUEAKS and catlike YEE-OW-OWLS!

His smaller friend is Bugaboo.

He loves to tease and torment too.

When clocks, at night,
begin to chime,
Bugaboo's "WOOOOO"
will chill your spine!

They're tricksters both—one tall, one small.
They don't care WHOOOO they scare at all.

They snicker.

They sneak.

They make their plans

while schemingly rubbing their hairy hands.

They shinny up trees and jiggle and jump.
Limbs SCRITCH-SCRATCH
and THUMP-BUMP-BUMP.

The children wake. What c-c-could it be?

They hear a faint "TEE-HEE-HEE-HEE!"

A CR-R-REAK! and SQUEAK! sound on the sill.

Their room grows dark, and d-d-darker still.

The children cry and all complain,
while grown-ups calmly try to explain.

There's nothing there—a moth, a breeze,
a house's creak, a mouse's sneeze.

Shadows—one, then two—appear!
When grown-ups look, they disappear!

All the clocks in town chime 'round.

Bugaboo wails his chilling sound.

Bugbear joins in with a H-OW-OWL
and an oh-so-scary catlike YEE-OW-OWL!

The children cry and all complain
of noises rattling their windowpane.

They sh-sh-shiver and shake and cover their heads and huddle down deep inside their beds.

The grown-ups blame the wind, a cat.
The children know it's more than that.

Bugbear laughs,
and Bugaboo, too,
for they love to, love to,
frighten you.

They snicker.

They sneak.

They make their plans

while schemingly rubbing their hairy hands.

They tilt the house and sh^ake shake shake.
Beds begin to quiver and quake!

The children cry and all complain,

while grown-ups calmly try to explain.

It's just a truck, a clackity train,
a thunderstorm, the ZOOOOOM of a plane.

Faces suddenly flash past!

The children know! They know at last!

It's not a truck!

It's not a train!

It's not a storm!

It's not a plane!

They see two tricksters land—*Kerplop!*
Now the children will . . . make . . . them . . . STOP!

They tiptoe (shhhhh!) across the floor.
They slip downstairs and out the door
and hide in hedges out of view,
then shout the loudest, scariest,

"BOO!!!!"

Bugbear JUMPS, and Bugaboo, too,
for they've never heard such a horrible "BOO!!!"

With hair on-end and popping eyes,
they jump,
they run,

they race,
they fly,

up the hill,
over the top,

down again,
. . . and never stop!

$16.00

DATE			